AWAKENING

☼

A CHRISTMAS EPISODE OF
THE STARTLIGHT CHRONICLES

A GRAPHIC NOVEL

☼

STORY BY
C. S. Johnson

ART BY
Eko Bambang

STORY AUTHOR
C. S. Johnson

ILLUSTRATOR
Eko Bambang

eBook ISBN: 978-1-948464-31-4
Print ISBN: 978-1-948464-32-1

For Sam.

Story adapted from *Awakening: A Christmas Episode of The Starlight Chronicles* by C. S. Johnson, part of the short story collection from The Starlight Chronicles. This book includes a sample chapter of *The Heights of Perdition,* Book 1 of The Divine Space Pirates.

OAHM...

....

BECAUSE OF A ROGUE
METEOR HITTING THE CITY
A FEW MONTHS PRIOR, ALL
THE PARTIES MY FRIENDS
PLANNED TO IMPRESS ME
(AND THE REST OF THE
STUDENT BODY) WERE
FORGONE. SO THIS YEAR
I WAS STUCK WITH MY
FAMILY.

BLAARRR!!!

zwwww......

IT WAS CHRISTMAS EVE, AND CHRISTMAS HAD NEVER BEEN REALLY GREAT FOR ME. THE ANNUAL HORRORS OF SHOPPING, THE ENDLESS SOUNDING OF THE SAME OLD SONGS, AND THE SOUND-OFF BETWEEN WINTER HOLIDAYS...SOMEHOW SANTA CLAUS EVEN MANAGED TO COME OFF AS A SORT OF VILLAIN, BRINGING GIFTS TO "GOOD CHILDREN–CORRUPTING THEIR EXPECTATIONS AND MOTIVES FOR LIFE–AND "PUNISHING" "BAD" CHILDREN WITH COAL, A MORE PRACTICAL GIFT IN THE EYES OF AN OVER-ECONOMICALLY CON-CERNED GENERATION. (YOU COULD AT LEAST BURN IT FOR WARMTH AND SAVE ON ENERGY BILLS.)

IT WAS ESPECIALLY BAD THIS PARTICULAR CHRISTMAS IN APOLLO CITY, OHIO, AND IT WASN'T BECAUSE OF THE WEATHER. FOR ONCE.

Hamilton Dinger

IF I, HAMILTON DINGER, THE TOP OF MY CLASS, A SUPER HOT, STAR ATHLETE, WORKING SECRETLY AS THE CITY'S VERY OWN PART-TIME VIGILANTE/HERO, COULD NOT HAVE WHAT I DESERVED, THEN WHAT CHANCE DID THE REST OF THE WORLD STAND ?

BLINKINGLY, I WATCHED GRANDPA ODD, WHO WAS POSSESSED WITH A VIGOR BELYING HIS ANCIENT YEARS, AS HE FINISHED RECITING FROM "THE META-MORPHOSIS" AND APPROACHED ME.

Rachel Cole

INSIDE OF BACKPACK WAS MY ONLY REASON FOR ENJOYING THIS CHRISTMAS-A PRESENT FOR MY HIGH-SCHOOL CRUSH, GWEN KESSLER. IT WAS ONE OF THOSE COSTLY, EXPENSIVE, "COCOA CHANNEL" CASHMERE SWEATERS. AND LET ME TELL YOU, IT HAD BEEN A PAIN AND A HALF TO GET.

I'D NEEDED TO GET MY MOTHER'S PERSONAL SHOPPER, JACQUES, ON BOARD, AND HE WASN'T EXCITED ABOUT DOING ME ANY FAVORS. (APPARENTLY HE WAS STILL ON PROBATION FROM THE CHRISTMAS DEBACLE FROM LAST YEAR. BUT IT WASN'T MY FAULT THE GIFTS WERE DESTROYED BY THE FIRE ALARM/SPRINKLER SYSTEM WHEN I'D SNEAKED IN LATE FROM A HOCKEY GAME WITH PONCEY, WHO, AS ONE OF MY USUALLY MORE PATHETIC FRIENDS, HAD REACHED A NEW LOW BY PRACTICALLY BEGGING ME TO GO).

SO I HAD TAKEN GREAT PAINS TO ASSURE JACQUES, FOR AT LEAST FIVE EXTRA MINUTES, I WOULD GET CHERYL TO REIN-STATE HIM. WHICH I HAD FORGOTTEN TO DO. COME TO THINK OF IT.

SURE. I'LL PACK THAT RIGHT UP FOR YOU

UGH. AS EXCITED AS I WAS THAT GWEN WAS ABLE TO HAVE ME OVER TO DELIVER HER PRESENT (HER FATHER HAS THIS RIDICULOUSLY HIGH STANDARD FOR BOYS. WELL, RIDICULOUS TO OTHER BOYS, I SUPPOSE; I ACTUALLY MET/EXCEEDED THE STANDARDS, NOT LIKE TIM RYDER, A SOCIALLY AWKWARD HALF-WIT, WHO'D ASKED GWEN OUT A FEW MONTHS AGO AND WAS PUT ON HOLD TILL GWEN'S SIXTEENTH BIRTHDAY) I DID NOT WANT TO LEAVE. IT MARKED THE BEGINNING OF THE END OF MY TIME AWAY FROM MY FAMILY.

SO, YOUNG HAMILTON, BACK AGAIN FOR SOME HOLIDAY CHEER?

GRANDPA ODD SAT NEXT TO ME WITH A GLOATING LOOK ON HIS FACE, AS IF HE KNEW HE WAS PRETTY MUCH IRRITATED ME AND ENJOYED DOING IT, AND EVEN SECRETLY KNEW IT FRUITLESS FOR ME TO COMPLAIN.

HEY, GRANDPA.

HERE

THEY LOOK BURNT

IT'S GINGERBREAD. THE MORE BURNT-LOOKING THE BETTER. AND THE CHOCOLATE CHIPS MAKE IT ALL THE SWEETER.

AH, AND THERE YOU GO

WHAT A TRANSFORMATION HOPE MAKES, ESPECIALLY AT THIS TIME OF YEAR!

WHAT ARE YOU TALKING ABOUT?

THE IRRITATING TWINKLE IN HIS AYE REMINDED ME I NEVER LIKED HIS ANSWERS TO MY QUESTIONS. THEY TENDED TO INCLUDE AN OBSCURE LITERARY REFERENCE AND THEN SOME KIND OF CRAZY REMARK. (RACHEL HAD TOLD ME BEFORE HE'D BEEN AN ENGLISH TEACHER. I NEVER QUESTIONED IT, BUT I FIGURED THAT WAS THE REASON HE WAS SO OLD AND STILL LIVING AT HOME WITH RACHEL AND HER OVERLY-OPINIONATED MOTHER, LETTY).

WHAT DO YOU THINK OF KAFKA'S METAMORPHOSIS?

I JUST FINISHED READING THAT FOR ENGLISH

YOU'RE TOO LATE TO HELP WITH THE HOMEWORK.

NO THAT I'D NEEDED THE HELP

SOME WORKAHOLIC, UNDER-APPRECIATED GUY HAD TRANSFORMED INTO A GIANT BUG AND MADE HIS FAMILY HATE HIM. HE'D ALSO LOST HIS JOB AND THE ABILITY TO SEND HIS SISTER TO MUSIC SCHOOL. TOUGH LIFE. I'LL BET NOBODY EVER WONDERED IF HE'D DESERVED IT

BUT EVEN IF HE DID, HE GREW HOPELESS AND DIED AS SUCH. HE WAS A BUG. ON THE OUTSIDE, HE WAS. INSIDE HE WAS HUMAN, LIKE YOU OR I.

DON'T MISTAKE ME, BOY. THIS TIME OF THE YEAR IS ALL ABOUT HOPE. DON'T MISS IT BECAUSE YOU'RE TOO PROUD. HOPE TRANSFORMS PEOPLE INTO NEW CREATIONS WE COULD NEVER BE WITHOUT IT.

I SIPPED UP THE LAST OF MY MOCHA TO HIDE MY DISCOMFORT. WHY SHOULD I HOPE FOR A GOOD CHRISTMAS?

I GLANCED DOWN AT THE BLACK, FOUR-POINT STAR MARKED ON THE INSIDE OF MY WRIST. IT WAS THE MARK WHICH SET ME APART FROM THE REST OF THE WORLD, A SUPERNATURAL MARK WHICH TRANSFORMED ME INTO MY SUPERHERO SELF; LIKE KAFKA'S VERMIN, IT WAS A TRANSFORMATION I DIDN'T KNOW IF I DESERVED OR NOT, AND ONE I DIDN'T WANT TO THINK ABOUT.

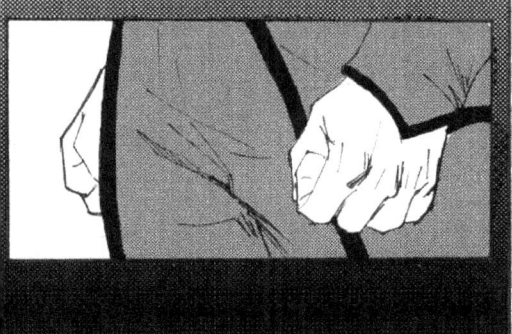

HOPE? THE IDEA OF HOPE MADE ME SNEER. BUT I SUPPOSE I WASN'T COMPLETELY HOPELESS.
I DID, AFTER ALL, HAVE GWEN'S PRESENT TO DELIVER. IT WAS A PERFECT SHADE FOR HER AUBURN HAIR AND HONEY BROWN EYES, SOME COLOR CALLED VANILLA MINT (THOUGHT IT WAS JUST LIGHT GREEN TO ME). NOT ONLY THAT, I'D SEEN A RESPECTABLE CELEBRITY WEARING IT.

I'D MADE SURE JACQUES BOUGHT THE FINEST ONE HE COULD BARGAIN FOR BY INDIRECTLY MENTIONING THE SECRET HE WAS KEEPING FROM MY BROTHER BAOUT HIS JOB. (I DIDN'T REALLY HAVE ANY DIRT ON HIM, BUT IF YOU ARE CONFIDENT AND VAGUE ENOUGH PEOPLE DO WHAT YOU WANT ANYWAY. YOU MIGHT THINK I AM PETTY, BUT IF HE WAS NERVOUS, YOU HAVE TO WONDER WHAT HE WAS HIDING). I'D EVEN HAD IT WRAPPED UP PROFESSIONALLY BY A MALL VOLUNTEER, AND PACKED IT ALONG WITH A CARD TELLING GWEN PRETTY MUCH THAT I, AS THE MOST CHARMING AND TALENTED GUY AT SCHOOL, WAS MEANT FOR HER. I HAD IT ON GOOD AUTHORITY GIRLS NEEDED A BUNCH OF GUSHY-FEELY DESCRIPTIONS LIKE THAT.

HERE'S YOUR ORDER.

WHAT ARE YOU SMILING ABOUT?

I WAS SMILLING?

JUST THINKING ABOUT GWEN. I GOT HER A GIFT, AND I'M GOING TO GO DELIVER IT TONIGHT

WHAT'S SO WRONG ABOUT SAYING THAT?

I GUESS BECAUSE IT'S YOU. YOU DON'T BELIEVE IN TRUE LOVE.

RACHEL AND I HAVE HAD THIS ARGUMENT SEVERAL TIMES, AND SHE WAS RIGHT TO SAY I DIDN'T BELIEVE IN TRUE LOVE, I.E. THE "THE ONE" CONSPIRACY, ETC. I COULD FRANKLY HAVE ANY GIRL I WANTED, REALLY. BUT GWEN WAS A GOOD FIT FOR ME. SHE WAS SMART, KIND, AND FUN. SHE WAS FUN TO PLEASE AND TO TEASE, AND IF SHE WAS ON THE LIST OF THE HOTTEST GIRLS IN SCHOOL, THAT WASN'T REALLY MY FAULT. IRRITATION FLASHED THROUGH ME; MY LAST CHANGE FOR HAPPINESS AT ALL FOR CHRISTMAS, AND HERE RACHEL WAS RUINING IT!

HERE, MERRY CHRISTMAS. TAKE IT; IT'S THE REST OF THE GINGERBREAD COOKIES

YOU SEEM TO ENJOY THEM A LOT

ANYTHING YOU MAKE IS ALWAYS GOOD, RACHEL.

THANKS, BUT THESE AREN'T ACTUALLY MINE

MY COUSIN MAKES THESE. GINGERBREAD IS HER SPECIALTY. MINE ARE NEVER AS GOOD AS HERS.

"OH". THANK GOODNESS THE BELOVED COOKIES WERE NOT NOT NOT FROM HER SENILE GRANDFATHER; I HAD A VISION OF HIM, MIXING HIS MEDS INTO THE COOKIE BATTER. OR MAYBE IT WAS LETTY, RACHEL'S DRAMA QUEEN OF A MOTHER, SPITTING INTO IT AND CALLING IT A "SECRET INGREDIENT"

YOU SHOULDN'T GIVE THEM AWAY THEN. SOMEONE ELSE MIGHT WANT THEM

NONSENSE. IF THEY BRING YOU JOY, YOU SHOULD HAVE THEM.

MEANWHILE, GRANDPA ODD FOUND HIS CHANNEL - OLD PEOPLE CENTRAL, THE LOCAL NEWS STATION

PIP!

...WARNING OF SUSPECTED ATTACKS... VARIOUS MAGAZINES...REPORTERS... BLOGGERS, AND... HAVE OFFERED A VARIETY OF REWARDS FOR AN INTERVIEW WITH THESE SO-CALLED SUPERHEROES, WINGDINGER AND STARRY KNIGHT.

OTHER SUBMISSIONS INCLUDE PICTURES... PROCEED WITH CAUTION... SAFETY FIRST... UNKNOWN

MY GAZE ONCE MORE SLIPPED DOWN TO MY WRIST

NAMES OF UNPLEASANT MEMORIES, THE TRIALS OF SUPERNATURAL WARFARE, STARRY KNIGHT, AND MY CHANGELING DRAGON HELPER/MENTOR/FREELOADING ROOMMATE ELYSIAN DRIFTED THROUGH MY MIND ALONG WITH THE IDEA OF GREGOR SAMSA. HOW LUCKY HE WAS!

HE DIDN'T HAVE A GROUP OF SIMILARLY TRANSFORMED FRIENDS WHO HELPED PURGE THE EARTH OF THE SINISTER-LINGS, THE MONSTERS OF EVIL FROM ANOTHER DIMENSION BENT ON WORLD DOMINATION, OR SOMETHING LIKE THAT (I WAS A BIT FUZZY ON THE DETAILS FROM ELYSIAN). CLENCHING MY FISTS, I HEADED OUT FOR THE NIGHT. IT WAS TIME TO GO MEET WITH GWEN.

THE APOLLO CITY TOWER CHIMED IN THE DISTANCE AS I WAVED GOODBYE TO RACHEL, ENJOYING THE SNOW EVEN AS I MISSED THE WARMTH OF THE CAFE'

ELYSIAN HAD TOLD ME ANY NUMBER OF THINGS ABOUT MY DESTINY. I WAS A FALLEN STAR, BUT A WARRIOR OF LIGHT. I HAD BEEN SENT TO EARTH TO FIGHT THE EVIL WHICH HAD JUST ARRIVED A FEW MONTHS AGO IN A CARE PACKAGE COURTESY OF AN OUTER DIMENSIONAL VERSION OF FEDEX, A LA THE METEOR WHICH HAD DESTROYED A GOOD PORTION OF MY CITY.

I WALKED THROUGH THE STREETS, HEADING OUT FOR GWEN'S HOUSE. IT WASN'T TOO FAR FROM MY SCHOOL, WHERE THE FIRST TIME I'D EVEN REALLY SEEN A SINISTER, MY ARCHNEMESIS, IN ALL OF THIS IMAGINARY GOOD-VERSUS-EVIL WAR.

ALTHOUGH WASN'T THAT IMAGINARY. BUT IT'S NOT LIKE I WOULD ADMIT THAT TO ANYONE. EVER.

BUT TO DO ALL THIS FIGHTING, OF COURSE, I HAD NO MEMORY OF MY POWER AS AN ASTRONESHAMA, AS ELYSIAN CALLED IT (IN "STAR LANGUAGE," NO LESS; I WAS STILL SKEPTICAL OF THAT), NO FORMAL TRAINING (OTHER THAN UNPLEASANT LECTURES AND SO-CALLED HINTS FROM ELYSIAN), AND STARRY KNIGHT, SOMEONE WHOM I'D ASSUMED WAS IN A POSITION LIKE MYSELF BUT WITHOUT THE ADDED BENEFIT OF A CHANGELING DRAGON SNARFING UP PERSONAL RESOURCES.

STARRY KNIGHT ANNOYED ME THE MOST. HOW COULD SOMEONE SO-BEAUTIFUL-I MEAN, SHE WAS OKAY-LOOKING FOR A WARRIOR. - BE SO IRRITATING?

I WALKED PAST A CHURCH AND MADE TO TURN WHEN I STOPPED SHORT. NORMALLY, MY EYES WOULD HAVE GLAZED RIGHT OVER IT, BUT SOMETHING STUCK OUT.

I WASN'T SURE WHAT IT WAS AT FIRST. A LOT OF CONSTRUCTION WORK NEEDED DONE BECAUSE OF METEORITE DAMAGE, OR SO I ASSUMED (I WAS CLOSE TO THE NORTHERN DISTRICT OF THE CITY, WHERE A LOT OF 'THE PROJECTS' REMAINED). A CROOKED SIGN IN THE YARD ANNOUNCED A DESPERATELY NEEDED COMMUNITY WORK DAY COMING UP. IT REALLY WASN'T THAT DIFFERENT FROM THE REST OF THE RUN-DOWN PARTS OF THE CITY.

A BUBBLE OF LIGHT WAS TWIRLING AROUND THE TREETOPS, FURTHER ENCIRCLED BY MANY OTHER LIGHTS. THEY WERE DANCING ABOVE THE USUAL FAKE LOOKING, RUN-DOWN MANGER SET UP

AS I WATCHED THE LIGHT MORE CLOSELY, THE BLURBY, BUBBLY OUTLINE WARPED INTO A HUMANLIKE FORM. I BLINKED BUT THERE WAS NO MISTAKING IT. IT WAS A BRIGHT AND SHINING STAR, FOLLOWED AROUND BY TEN OR SO FLITTY LITTLE LIGHTS.

AH!!!

KYAAA...!!!

ROOAARR!!!

KYAAAA!!!

!!!

PLEASE! HELP MY BABY!

I HAD A CHOICE TO MAKE. ONE: HELP FIGHT OFF THE DEMON. TWO: KEEP MY HEAD DOWN AND KEEP HEADING OFF TO GWEN'S. IT WAS CHRISTMAS EVE, AND THAT WAS HORRIBLE ENOUGH; I WANTED NOTHING MORE THAN TO KEEP WALKING. BUT AS I WATCHED, THE AIRY DARKNESS CAME TOGETHER IN MONSTER FORM AND PLUCKED A LITTLE FAIRY/BABY-STAR RIGHT OUT OF THE SKY.
A MOMENT OF ETERNITY STRETCHED AS THE MOTHER STAR HEARTBREAKINGLY CRIED OUT. ALL OF A SUDDEN THE CHASE WAS ON. THE DARKENED SPECTER FLED WITH HIS PRIZE; THE STAR SOARED ON AFTER HIM, HER OTHER CHILDREN CLOSE BEHIND HER, THEIR LITTLE VOICES SHRILLY WITH RIGHTEOUS ANGER.

HUA HAA HAA HAA

KYAAAA!!!

KYAAAA!!! KYAAAA!!!

BRAKKK!!!

BYURRR

WHAT IS THIS?

IT'S CHAI

THE GIRL BEGAN TO PICK UP HER FALLEN THINGS. I BARELY PAID ATTENTION TO HER AS I GRABBED AT MY BACKPACK. DESPAIR CLUNG TO ME. GWEN'S PRESENT! UGH. DEPRESSION AND THEN ANGER FLUSHED THROUGH ME.

NO! NO! NO! IT'S ALL WET!

Raiya

ONCE MORE, CHASING AFTER THE DEMONS HAD BROUGHT DISASTER UPON ME. FROM FAR AWAY, THE LITTLE IMP'S CAPTURED CRIES STILL CALLED TO ME. I HUNG MY HEAD. I STILL HAD A JOB TO DO. I'D HAVE TO WORRY ABOUT GWEN'S SWEATER LATER.

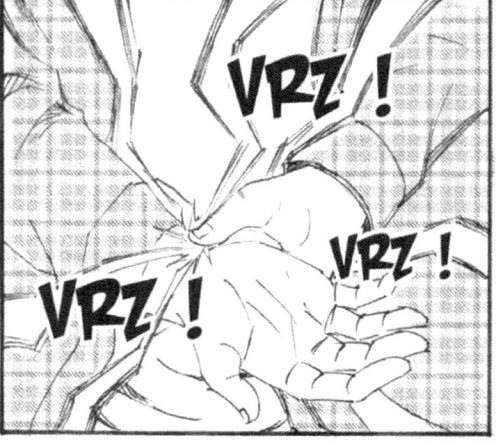

BUZZZ !!!

CRINK !

FWOOSS...

LAKE ERIE

HOP!

WUSS!

WUSS!!

TWACK!

!!!

GRAB !!!

AAA
AAAR
GHH
!!!

WHHCZZ !!!

SRETTT...

VZZZZ...

AH!

DHUAAARRR!!!

AAAA AAKK KHHH !!!

ELYSIAN HAD ARRIVED

GROOOOAAA...

BLEGARR...!!!

AAARRGGHHH

SSSSSS....

GLAD YOU COULD MAKE IT AT LAST

I HAD TO WAIT UNTIL YOU WERE FREE OF HIM, KID. UNLESS YOU WANTED ME TO BURN YOU TOO?

JUST GET DOWN HERE AND PICK ME UP, WOULD YOU!?

WUSS

WUSS

WUSS

HOPP!

ALL RIGHT, HOW DO WE DEFEAT THIS GUY?

WHICH ONE IS IT?

I DON'T KNOW. ALL I KNOW FOR SURE IS THAT IT'S A DESTROYER SINISTER

KNOW THE NAME, AND YOU WILL KNOW HOW TO DEFEAT IT. EVERYONE HAS A WEAKNESS.

WUSS WUSS WUSS

IT WAS TRYING TO DESTROY THAT STAR

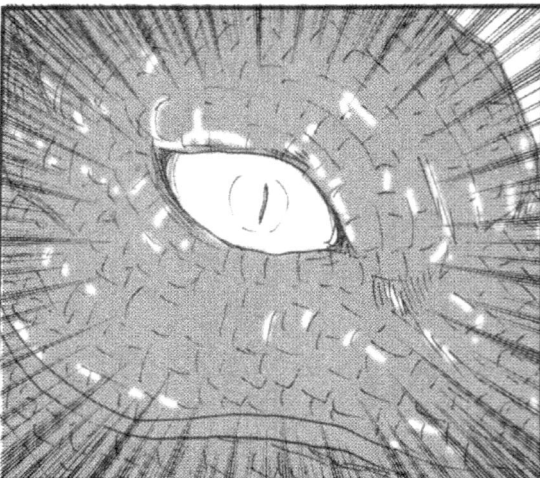

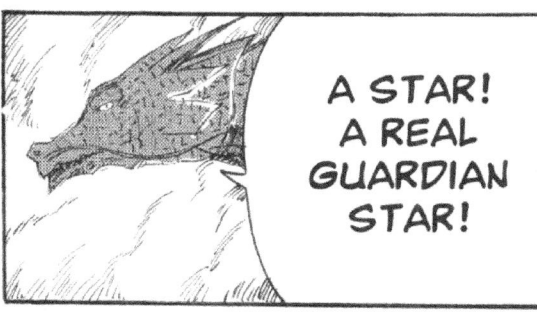

A STAR! A REAL GUARDIAN STAR!

WHAT?

KID, DO YOU KNOW HOW MANY STARLIGHT WARRIORS ARE ALLOWED TO BE ON EARTH IN THEIR PHYSICAL FORM? PRACTICALLY NONE!

BATS!

WUCHS!!

SLAPP!

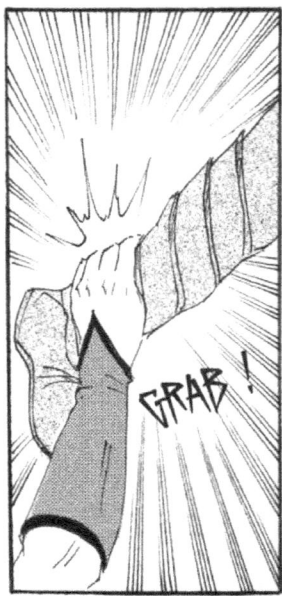

GRAB!

YASHOOL!!!

CRAP!

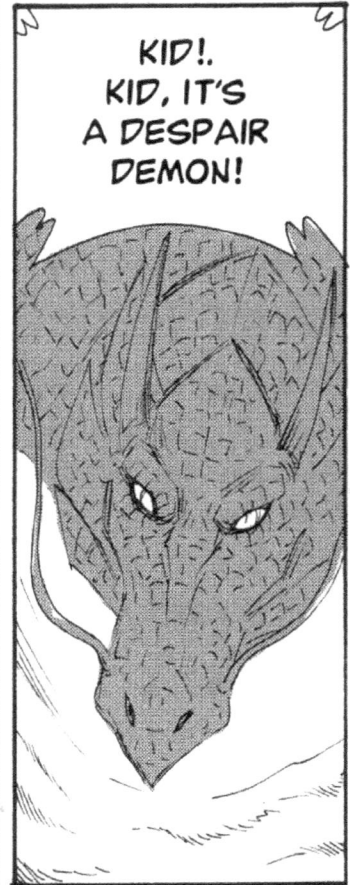

KID!. KID, IT'S A DESPAIR DEMON!

HRAAAAAAA!!!

WHAT?

IT'S A DESPAIR DEMON! IT THRIVES ON HOPELESSNESS!

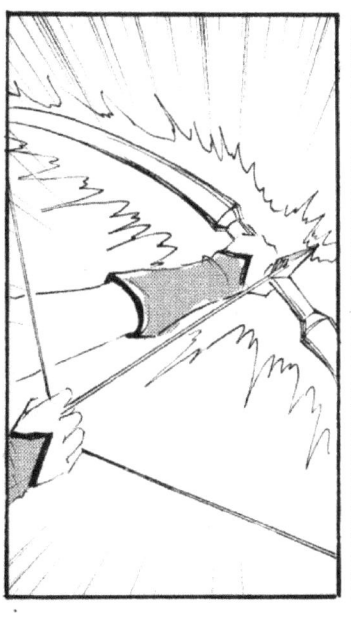

HERE!

PUNCH IT RIGHT THERE!

WHY?

IT'LL DESTROY IT, THAT'S WHY, IDIOT!

DHUAAAR!!!

BLEGAARRR!!!

SSSS....

SSSS....

THANK YOU FOR SAVING ME!

SURE. NO NEED TO THANK ME

YES, BECAUSE YOU STILL DON'T HAVE WHAT IT TAKES TO DO THIS JOB RIGHT. YOU PROBABLY ALMOST GOT HER KILLED

EXCUSE ME, BUT DIDN'T I JUST HELP YOU DEFEAT A MONSTER YOU COULDN'T FINISH ON YOUR OWN?

CHILDREN, ENOUGH.

I SEE YOU HAVEN'T CHANGED, STAR OF MERCY, AND YOU EITHER, STAR OF JUSTICE.

I SEE YOU STILL LIKE TO ARGUE

WE ARE KNOWN AS WINGDINGER AND STARRY KNIGHT IN THIS WORLD, LADY HOPE.

EITHER WAY, I MUST THANK YOU BOTH FOR THE RESCUE OF MY LITTLE ONE

WHO ARE YOU?

I AM ELPECE, THE STAR OF HOPE. EVERY CHRISTMAS I COME DOWN TO EARTH AND CELEBRATE. THIS YEAR THE SINISTERS HAVE NOT FAILED TO DO THE SAME, I SEE

FOR SAVING MY BELOVED, I WILL GRANT YOU EACH A WISH

YOU CAN REALLY DO THAT?

YEAH, I ONLY THOUGHT GENIES COULD DO THAT

EVERY STAR IS ONLY SUPPOSED TO HAVE ONE WISH

NOT ALL OF US ARE CREATED THE SAME, JUSTICE ... STARRY KNIGHT,

I AM ALLOWED TO GRANT WISHES, BUT THEY ARE NOT WISHES OF YOUR CHOOSING. THEY ARE MORE LIKE GIFTS, I SHOULD SAY, BUT MUCH MORE THAN GIFTS

I FIGURED THERE WAS A CATCH

I'D THOUGHT ABOUT ASKING HER TO FIX GWEN'S SWEATER UP FOR ME SINCE IT WAS ALL RUINED. SHE PROBABLY WOULDN'T DO THAT.

HERE IS THE WISH I GRANT FOR YOU, WINGDINGER: YOU WILL DO GREAT THINGS FOR YOUR CITY, EVEN THOUGH YOUR POWERS HAVE BEEN A BURDEN TO YOU. I GRANT YOU THE WISH OF CERTAINTY

HA.. HA.. HAA..

NO MATTER THE PATH YOU CHOOSE, YOU WILL BE GREAT AMONG MEN

THANKS. OH WELL. I HADN'T BEEN EXPECTING ANYTHING ANYWAY. NO LOSS.

LADY HOPE THEN TURNED TO STARRY KNIGHT, WHO SHOOK HER HEAD AND STEPPED BACK

THERE IS NO POINT, LADY HOPE. I KNOW FULL WELL THE CONSEQUENCES OF MY CHOICES

IT IS CHRISTMAS TIME, LADY JUSTICE, AND MY WISH IS YOUR GIFT, AND IT IS GOOD OF ME TO GIVE IT. I GRANT YOU THE GIFT OF DOUBT. YOU MUST KNOW THERE IS STILL A CHANCE FOR ALL YOU WISH TO COME TRUE

HOPE INDEED. FALSE HOPE, I WOULD SAY, BUT I KNOW YOU TOO WELL

YOU ARE NOT ABOVE THE PRINCE OF STARS, HE HAS SPOKEN ON THE SUBJECT, BUT YOU HAVE NOT FALLEN BEYOND HOPE. I WOULD BE THE ONE TO KNOW

I DIDN'T KNOW WHAT THEY WERE TALKING ABOUT AT THE TIME, BUT I WAS BORED AND TOO TIRED TO PAY ATTENTION. I WANTED TO GO SEE GWEN. ACTUALLY, I WANTED TO GO HOME AND SLEEP, IT'D BEEN AN EXHAUSTING NIGHT AND MY CHRISTMAS GIFT WAS RUINED

LADY HOPE SMILED BRIGHTLY. "FAREWELL, PEACE ON EARTH, AND GOODWILL TOWARDS MEN!" THEN SHE AND HER CHARGES SHOT AWAY INTO THE NIGHT, LEAVING US TO OURSELVES ONCE MORE. STARRY KNIGHT TURNED AND BEGAN WALKING AWAY.

ALL SHE DID WAS COMPLIMENT ME, WHAT A RIP

SHE DID NOT JUST GIVE YOU WORDS, KID. SHE GAVE YOU HOPE. GOODNESS KNOWS YOU NEEDED IT, YOU ARE ALMOST HOPELESS SOME DAYS.

MY "WISH" HAD SUCKED. HERS PROBABLY HAD, TOO.

HEY!

WHAT?

HERE, MERRY CHRISTMAS, SORRY IF THEY ARE A BIT CRUMBLED.

WHAT...?

CHOCOLATE CHIP GINGER-BREAD. THEY'RE MY NEW FAVORITE. I NEVER THOUGHT I WOULD LIKE THESE, BUT I DO.

THANK YOU

GOTTA BE BETTER THAN HOPE'S GIFT, RIGHT?

IT IS ABOUT THE SAME, REALLY

WERE YOU HOPING I WOULD QUIT?

THAT'S NONE OF YOUR BUSINESS!

BUT YOU SHOULD QUIT ANYWAY

SO I WAS RIGHT!

CAN'T YOU JUST LEAVE ME ALONE?

CAN'T YOU JUST LEAVE ME ALONE?

A NUMBER OF THINGS HAPPENED IN THE NEXT SEVERAL MOMENTS. ELYSIAN BUMPED ME, TRYING TO TELL ME ABOUT MY CELL PHONE, WHICH HAD BEEN RINGING OFF THE HOOK (GWEN CALLING TO ASK WHERE I WAS.) I RESIGNED MYSELF AS STARRY KNIGHT FINALLY JUMPED OFF AND FLEW AWAY; DESPITE OUR ARGUMENTS I NOTICED THAT SHE KEPT THE COOKIES TIGHTLY IN HER CLUTCHES ... PROBABLY TO SPITE ME. I TURNED MY ATTENTIONS TO ELYSIAN, WHO, UNWILLING AND OFFENDED BY MY DESIRE TO ARGUE AND CALL HIM NAMES, LEFT ME BEHIND TO WALK HOME. AFTER CURFEW, IN THE MIDDLE OF THE NIGHT.

SOON AFTER, I HEARD THE CLOCK TOWER CHIME IN THE DISTANCE.
IT WAS MIDNIGHT. CHRISTMAS DAY.
AND REGARDLESS OF MYSELF, I SMILED AS I BEGAN HEADING TO MY
HOUSE. IT WAS THE FIRST YEAR IN A LONG TIME CHRISTMAS MEANT
SOMETHING GOOD. EVEN IF I WASN'T SURE JUST YET WHAT IT WAS
THAT WAS SO GOOD.
I STILL HAD TO FIGURE OUT THE REASONS FOR MY SUPERNATURAL
TRANSFORMATION. BUT LADY HOPE'S GIFT AND THE BATTLE TONIGHT
HAD GIVEN ME SOMETHING BETTER THAN CERTAINTY. I WOULDN'T CALL
IT HOPE, BUT WHEN I THOUGHT ABOUT HOW GOOD IT'D FELT TO GIVE
STARRY KNIGHT A PRESENT, I WAS AT A LOSS FOR A BETTER WORD.
EVEN AS I LISTENED TO GWEN'S VOICEMAILS (WHICH MOVED
FROM GRADUAL CONCERN OVER BEING LATE TO CHEWING ME OUT FOR
STANDING HER UP), AND RUMPLED OUT THE RUINED CHRISTMAS
SWEATER, LIFE FELT MORE MYSTICAL AND REAL, MORE HOPEFUL AND
FRIGHTENING. LIKE MY LIFE WAS MORE CONNECTED AND DEEPLY
ROOTED IN SOMETHING GRAND AND MEANINGFUL.
I SNORTED DISDAINFULLY AT THE THOUGHT; APPARENTLY MY
CYNICISM HAD BEEN ERODED, EVER SO SLIGHTLY.
OH WELL, I MUSED, WALKING PAST THE CHURCH AGAIN. STRANGER
THINGS HAVE HAPPENED. I WAS CERTAIN OF THAT AT LEAST.

C. S. Johnson is the author of several young adult
sci-fi and fantasy novels, including *The Starlight Chronicles* series, the *Once Upon a Princess* saga, and the *Divine Space Pirates* trilogy. With a gift for sarcasm and an apologetic heart, she currently lives in Atlanta with her family.

Please read on for a sample of *The Heights of Perdition*, the first book in The Divine Space Pirates Trilogy, a science fiction romance series from C. S. Johnson.

In an apocalyptic future, Aerie St. Cloud and Exton Shepherd were on opposing sides. But after their accidental encounter, their lives—and the lives of their friends, family, and nations—will never be the same.

Chapter 1 from

THE HEIGHTS

OF

PERDITION

BOOK ONE OF *THE DIVINE SPACE PIRATES*

♦♦♦♦

C. S. Johnson

♦ 1 ♦

At just the right angle, the dark blue and white orb, suspended in a sea of invisible shadows, held in place by a faith as impossible to believe in as it was to see, fit nicely between his fingers. Outside his window, Earth looked small and fragile, seemingly innocent, and mostly harmless. A hollowness slipped between his thumb and forefinger as he squashed them together, crushing the blueberry-sized circle.

Amused by the irony of the forced perspective before him, a rare, genuine smile formed on Exton Shepherd's face.

It was, he decided, almost a shame no one else was around to witness such an unusual event. He smooshed his fingers together, imagining the world completely decimated into dust.

But then, he recalled, he'd given plenty of smiles earlier, as all the hubbub went on about the ship. Surely the crew, his hodgepodge of adopted family and coworkers, would have been satisfied with those, even though they were inauthentic at best and mocking at worst.

Duty sometimes demanded playing happy. Exton knew that, and he followed it, even in instances he loathed.

Like today.

Between the thirteenth and fifteenth sunrises of his day, he'd watched the only other person he truly cared for in all the world—no, he mentally corrected himself, in all the universe—pledge her love, heart, and life to another man.

It was heartbreaking on some levels, but strangely freeing, too.

The wedding had been quaint, warm, and sweet. Its simplicity suggested nothing of its socially taxing nature.

Exton had no regrets about ducking out as soon as the bride and groom finished their vows and the Ecclesia had pronounced them husband and wife.

Once he had successfully slipped out of sight, Exton proceeded to the Captain's Lounge, the small room he'd claimed as his the day after launching the *Perdition* into space. There was little to be said of the room's comfort; it was more like a tall elevator shaft than a room, empty of everything but the coldness of space and a small window hidden up near the far end. More than once, Exton wondered if he'd found a kind of kinship with it; hollow and bleak, with a tiny view looking out toward the fleeing horizon.

It was there, on a window seat built into the windowpane, where Exton tucked his legs under his chin and entered into his own world of privacy, where he was free to be who he wanted, even if it was for only a moment.

As captain of the ship, he didn't want his crew to see him in one of his more melancholy moods.

His frown returned when he opened his fingers again, only to see Earth was still hanging in space before him, its silence mocking and spiteful. Rearranging his hand, he made it seem like he was carrying the earth in the palm. Fleetingly, he toyed with the idea of pretending to toss the small pearl away into the dark recesses of space, into an imaginary hell.

But he knew that would not work.

Exton knew two things with startling clarity and unshakable certainty: The first was that hell was real, and the second was that it was his home.

"Having fun?" a voice asked from below him.

"Huh?" Exton jerked around in surprise, nearly falling off the window ledge. "Come on, Emery, don't do that," he groaned, while the young woman dressed all in white only laughed. His balance, already compromised by the pull of the starship's gravity, faltered again as Exton tried to adjust himself. "You know I don't like it when people interrupt me, especially when I'm here."

"But it's my wedding day," Emery insisted. "And I'd like to have a dance with the ship's captain before the night shift starts. Come on, we're up first."

Exton gave up on staying by the window and jumped down as gracefully as he could. "All the shifts up here are technically the night shift," he grumbled.

"Some would say we live in perpetual day up here on the *Perdition*," Emery offered, her voice gentle even as she maintained her stance. "Sunrise and sunset are only ninety-two minutes apart for us now, when we're this close to Earth."

"Sunrises and sunsets do not make day and night up here," Exton told her, touching his forehead.

Emery reached out and took his hand, before she placed it over his heart. "I think your problem is too much night in here, not out there." She turned her attention back to the window, where six inches of steel-grade glass separated them from the vacuum of space.

Exton followed her gaze, wondering if she was looking for any sign of familiarity from their old home. He watched as the end of the ocean braced itself against the shore of the Old Republic; he felt his memory pull him in, and he could see it clearly inside his mind.

The chill of the old mountains where he would go work and play with his father, the spray of the salt water on his transport module, the warmth of his mother's arms as she welcomed him home from school—all of it embraced him, surrounding him and penetrating into the deep recesses of his heart.

And then there was pain, and then it was gone.

Exton shook his head. "I know it seems like a long time has passed, but it's time to cause the URS some trouble. It's almost the anniversary, you know."

"I know," she replied. A sudden sadness appeared in her gaze, and Exton wondered if she had been reminiscing as well.

Pushing aside his grief, he straightened his shoulders. "I have a plan that will really make them sorry this year, Em."

"I know you're a man of your word," Emery replied, "but I'm not sure it will be enough to convince them to give us what we want."

"They already cannot give us what we want." Exton shrugged. "Our game was never for power. It was for meaning."

"It's not a game, Exton."

"I know it's not!" Out of the corner of his eye, he saw Emery flinch. "I know it's not," he repeated carefully, reverting to his usual, detached tone. "It's not our fault that it became a quest for survival, Emery. I know that even more than you do."

"If it's survival you want," Emery scoffed, "there's no point in selling your soul in the process."

Before Exton could assure Emery he had no soul left that was worth saving, let alone selling, he stopped. Happy times, he reminded himself.

Emery's wedding was a special occasion, one that had excited her for the past several months, offering a glimmer of hope on a horizon of gloom and turmoil. Exton was determined not to let the past rob him—or her—of anything else, so long as it was in his power. "You're right," he acquiesced, momentarily giving in.

Emery smiled brightly, and Exton suddenly had a hard time believing she was only two years younger than he was. At twenty-two, she seemed much more innocent than the figure that gazed back at him when he looked in the mirror.

He slipped his hand out from under hers, before taking and squeezing it. "Are you sure you wouldn't like to have the first dance with your new husband?"

"Tyler is my heart's desire," Emery told him firmly, "but you will always be my hero."

Exton grimaced. He knew he was no hero. "It would be a shame to waste your time with me."

"Time with you is not a waste."

"Did Tyler approve of changing up the dancing order? The man might be in love, but there's no need to make him prove to be the fool."

"Hey, Tyler's your commander, and your best friend," Emery objected. "You know he's not a fool."

"Not where it concerns you. He would be smart to correct that, and I have been telling him since he received approval from the Ecclesia to start courting you," Exton told her. He gave her a devious look. "Should I make him walk the plank?"

Emery frowned and searched the darkened shadows of his face. "That's not funny, Exton."

"I know."

They walked in silence for a few moments before Exton spoke once more. "I don't want to dance. No offense, Em."

"Traditionally, it was the daughter's duty to dance with her father, first." Emery smiled. "But that's more of a cultural thing I've read about from the Old Republic."

"Yes, I remember that," Exton agreed. "Ironic, how the Revolutionary States would be appalled by it now."

Of course, he recalled, even the idea of using the term "father" might have some of the more militant protestors up in arms, as the beloved Daddy Dictator of the URS, Grant Osgood, did not encourage familial relationships, unless such feelings were directed toward government.

"If the URS is against it, you should be more inclined to appease me, then," Emery contended.

There was a breath of silence and stillness before Exton responded. "I'm not our father," he scoffed.

"You're more like him than you might wish."

As Exton scowled at her, Emery pointed her finger at him accusingly. "See? You even have the same exasperated look he used to get when he was frustrated."

"I'll have to take your word for it." Exton shrugged, scratching his head. He frowned as he realized it had been some time since he'd gotten a haircut. His father used to do the same thing, especially when he was planning his next engineering endeavor. Exton suddenly wondered if it was his own scruffy locks that had been making him shrink back from mirrors of late.

He missed his father too much to want to see him staring out of the mirror from the other side of the grave.

Emery chuckled again, drawing him out of his thoughts. "Well, I know at least one trait you share with him. He had a hard time telling me no to anything I wanted, if memory serves."

"You look too much like Mom for me to say no," Exton admitted. "I'm sure he had the same problem, but that's one I'm more willing to share with him."

With her dark brown hair, blue-green eyes, and petite form, Emery was the living memory of their mother. She even had the same dimple hovering above the left corner of her lips, a trait Exton knew was the extent of their common features. Their father's blue eyes, as clear and sharp as ice, had passed to him, along with his height, broad shoulders, and black hair.

"He always did want me to follow in his footsteps," Exton muttered as they headed out of the Captain's Lounge. "But I'm not sure he would have enjoyed the ghost of Captain Chainsword, the infamous space lumberjack pirate."

"I don't think he would have liked it, given how much he derided you for enjoying those fantasy adventures you used to read."

"It seemed fitting at the time, to create a new role for him to play, along with the rest of us."

"I suppose." Emery shrugged. "But Papa was a brilliant engineer, same as you, and a good man. I'm not sure he would have liked your emphasis on piracy and power."

"For the most part, I think you are right," Exton agreed. "But he was too idealistic by far. That was what got him killed." He looked out a nearby window, where, even as he could no longer see Earth, he still felt the pull of its shadow.

"In hindsight, you would prove to be correct on that point."

"That is why I will not make the same mistake as he did. While *Paradise* is out of reach, *Perdition* will do what it can to ensure a better life for us."

"And others, too," Emery added proudly.

"Maybe." Exton shrugged. "I only have a duty to you, and you're technically Tyler's problem now. Anyone else is just extra."

"Your duty to me hasn't ended."

Exton rolled his eyes. "I'm going to dance with you, aren't I? What else is there?"

"Your duty to me might include a dance tonight, but I wish for you to find someone you would love as I love Tyler." She smiled. "Someone you can spend your life trying to make happy."

"Even as life makes me miserable?"

Emery frowned and sighed. "I don't know why you do that."

"Do what?"

"Make it impossible for yourself to be happy."

"Happiness is fleeting, remember?" Exton rolled his eyes. "Even the leaders of the Ecclesia would agree with me there."

"They don't often agree with you, especially when it comes to your mandates," Emery concurred. "The only reason they would on this account is because the phrasing is vague enough to seem to agree on the meaning." She narrowed her gaze. "And the practice."

Exton wrinkled his nose. "We've been up here for too long if you know me so well."

"I still prefer this to when we were off at different universities, working on our studies," Emery admitted with a thoughtful smile. "But as for the argument, you don't seem to agree with the Ecclesia a whole lot, either. You don't share most of their beliefs. I find it hard to believe that you would try to garner support from among their teachings."

"Their teachings on wisdom and life, and how it should be, I respect. But it's different when you're trying to manage a pirate starship and ruin an empire."

"Not to mention when you insist so stubbornly on remaining miserable."

"I *am* going back to your wedding celebration, aren't I?" Exton groaned. "Please don't push it, Em. You know how I feel. If God would grant your wish for me, if he wanted so much for me to be 'happy,' he could have let me 'fall in love' with someone on the *Perdition*, like you and Tyler. But even when we send our smaller ships down to Earth for supplies, see Aunt Patty, or attack the URS, there's no one there for me. There are only people there who want the protection *Perdition* can offer to political dissents or refugees such as themselves."

After a moment of thought, he added, "Besides, my job is to protect and lead aboard the spaceship. The last thing I need is to be led around by the whims of a woman."

"There's no need to make it sound so deplorable," Emery scoffed, arching an eyebrow at him. "Do you honestly think dealing with the moods of a man are any easier?"

He flashed her a charming grin.

"You don't need to set yourself up for failure like that. We have only been up in space for six years now, hiding in the shadows of all the toxic clouds while playing war games with the URS."

"Not to mention watching destruction of all other sorts go unchecked," Exton added, his voice grim.

"It's not all 'unchecked,'" Emery reminded him. "Exton, you still can't lose hope. God is a supposed to be a god of miracles, remember? We have time."

Exton wondered how his sister could be worried about his heart, when his life, as well all the lives of his crew, faced the bigger risk. It was one thing to be aware of danger, but another to disregard it, especially for something as silly as true love.

He studied Emery's daydreaming smile in silence and decided he had the right of it: As much as she was ever his practical and precise sister, Emery's wedded bliss was affecting her judgment.

Exton was surprised at the sudden stab of jealousy. He squashed it down as he caught sight of the approaching Earth through the galley windows.

Didn't Emery see the coming battle? Exton wondered. *Didn't she feel the haunted air about the starship, with specters of the past lurking around every corner of the* Perdition?

They couldn't outlast the URS forever up in space. While Exton and the Ecclesia had established the *Perdition* as a safe haven over the past few years, it was only a matter of time before the URS would come for them, and he knew it would not be to make peace.

"What is it, Exton?" Emery asked, jolting him out of his gloomy thoughts.

Exton sighed. "It's not like God's just going to dump someone into the ship just for me. You might as well save your breath for dancing, Em."

Thank you for reading! Please leave a review for this book and check out www.csjohnson.me for other books and updates!